Bow wow!

For Edward and Anna ~ H.W.
For Lucy and James ~ K.P.

WOOF

Magazine

STRIPES PUBLISHING
An imprint of Magi Publications
1 The Coda Centre,
189 Munster Road,
London SW6 6AW

A paperback original
First published in Great Britain in 2012

ISBN: 978-1-84715-227-5

A CIP catalogue record for this book is available from the British Library.

Printed and bound in the UK.

10 9 8 7 6 5 4 3 2 1

For more information about Holly Webb visit:
www.holly-webb.com

My Naughty Little Puppy

HOLLY WEBB

stripes

Chapter One

The Doggy Bag

"Have you got everything you need to take to Lucy's house?" Mum came out of the kitchen to see Ellie struggling down the stairs so laden down with bags she looked like a packhorse. "What's all that? You're only going for the night!"

"My school bag, my sleeping bag and clothes for tomorrow, that's all," Ellie protested. "Um, please will you help me carry it to school?"

"I'll have to. You haven't even got your lunch yet!" Mum sighed. "Leave it all here, and come and have breakfast. Lila and Max are halfway through theirs. And where's Rascal? He hasn't turned up wanting his breakfast yet."

Rascal came down the stairs after Ellie. He was still such a small dog that he almost had to jump from step to step, but this morning he didn't seem to be bouncing down the way he usually did.

Ellie turned round and looked at Rascal anxiously. "I think he's a bit confused. He doesn't know why I've been packing. Do you think he'll be all right without me tonight, Mum? I haven't been on any sleepovers since we got him."

"It's only one night. I'm sure he'll be fine." Mum lifted Ellie's rucksack off her shoulder. "Honestly, Ellie, how many outfits have you got in here?" She unzipped it and looked inside. "You don't need your dressing gown! Or *three* cardigans. Put those on the stairs, I'll take them up later. Come on!"

Ellie followed her into the kitchen for breakfast, and Rascal trotted after them. He wolfed down his breakfast and wandered back out into the hallway. But when Ellie, Lila and Max went to put their coats on, he was nowhere to be seen.

"Where is he?" Ellie looked around. Now she thought about it, Rascal hadn't been sitting at her feet during breakfast, waiting for her to drop him bits of toast, which was very unusual. She put her lunch box on top of her rucksack, so she could go and check upstairs.

Her rucksack squeaked, and Ellie turned round in surprise. It was wriggling as well. She lifted her lunch box up again, and Rascal poked his head out of the bag, looking cross.

Max shook his head. "I can't believe he wants to go to school. You can go instead of me, Rascal. I've got a French test. It's not fair! Tests shouldn't be allowed on Fridays!"

"Oh, Rascal." Ellie lifted the little Jack Russell out of her rucksack and hugged him. "I'll see you tomorrow. I'll be home after lunch. It won't be that long, honestly."

She was trying not to sound worried, but it was difficult. What if he really missed her? When they'd first got him, Rascal had made Mum's life a misery while Ellie was at school, howling and scratching at the doors. Luckily, their dog-training instructor, Jo, had suggested giving him a cardigan of Ellie's to have in his basket so he wouldn't miss her, and it had worked. But Rascal still raced to the door to meet Ellie after school, if Mum hadn't brought him with her to pick Ellie up. And if she went to tea with one of her friends, Lila and Max had told her that he would sniff them disappointedly, and then go and sulk in his basket till she came home. How was he going to behave now that she was away for a day and a half?

"Ellie, he'll be fine," Mum told her firmly. "You worry about him too much. Let's go."

Ellie nodded, but as Mum shut the front door, she was sure she could hear Rascal whining sadly.

When Ellie got to school, Christy and Lucy were at the gate waiting for her, looking excited. Sorting Rascal out had made Ellie a bit late, so they hardly had any time to talk about Lucy's sleepover before school, but as soon as the bell went for break, they dashed out to grab one of the benches, where they could sit and plan.

"Mum says we can go to the DVD shop on the way home from my dance class," Lucy told them. She looked anxiously from Ellie to Christy. "You're sure you don't mind coming to watch it? It might be a bit boring."

"Lucy! We've said loads of times we don't mind!" Ellie told her. "It'll be fun. You were brilliant dancing in the Christmas play, I'd love to watch a class."

Lucy smiled. "I would have missed it, but I've only just started stage dancing."

"Is it different to ballet?" Christy asked.

"Really different!" Lucy nodded. "It's a bit of acting, and a bit of dance, and some singing. Last week Miss Louisa, our teacher, said there was going to be something exciting at the next class, but it's going to be a surprise. Maybe someone's coming to dance for us. Miss Louisa knows lots of dancers from musicals."

"What are we going to do tomorrow morning?" Ellie asked.

Lucy smiled. "Well, I've got a plan." She looked hopefully at Ellie and Christy, as though she wanted them to ask her what it was.

Ellie stared at her. "What sort of plan?"

Lucy started to undo her school bag, and Christy pounced, seeing the shiny covers of some magazines poking out. "*Animal Time* magazine! And the new issue of *Pet Planet*! Are you going to get a pet?" she asked excitedly. "What are you getting? A dog?"

Lucy shook her head.

"No. We did think about it when we came to the Christmas Fair – we even wondered if we could get one from Paws for Thought. But then we decided it wouldn't be fair. I've got dance classes at the weekend, and we wouldn't be able to go for really long walks like you two do with Bouncer and Rascal. And I'm still a bit nervous around some dogs, especially big ones. But I would like some sort of pet. I need you two to help me work out what. And then we have to convince my mum! She sort of liked the idea of a dog, but I suggested a pet mouse to her the other day, and she wasn't happy!"

Ellie nodded thoughtfully. It was a pity that Lucy couldn't adopt a dog from an animal shelter like Paws for Thought. The girls had all recently helped out at a Christmas Fair to raise money for the shelter. But it was very exciting that Lucy was getting a pet. Ellie frowned a little, remembering Rascal. She really hoped he was going to be all right without her.

Chapter Two

A Surprise for Lucy

"I wonder what the special exciting thing's going to be?" Christy whispered. Ellie shrugged. She and Christy were sitting with Lucy's mum at the edge of the dance studio, where there were a few chairs for parents. Lucy and the rest of her dance class were working on a complicated routine to a song from *The Wizard of Oz*, and it was fun to watch. But no one had mentioned the surprise yet.

"Maybe someone from the show is coming to dance for them? It's on in London at the moment, isn't it?"

Christy nodded. "Could be that."

"Is it OK if I get a drink of water?" Ellie asked Lucy's mum. There was a water cooler by the door to the studio. Lucy's mum nodded, and Ellie crept along the side of the room, trying not to disturb the dancers.

As she went back to her seat, Ellie noticed a man and a woman sitting close to the water cooler. They were watching the girls dancing, and the man was making notes on a clipboard.

"Yes, the one with the curly dark hair," the woman was saying, as Ellie walked past. "She's a definite. Such a lovely smile, and she's got real stage presence."

Dark hair – Ellie glanced across at the girls dancing. Lucy was the only one with really curly dark hair. Quickly she looked back at the clipboard, which had a logo on the back. Eclipse Productions. Was it a TV company? And it sounded like they were interested in Lucy! She hurried back to her seat, and whispered her news to Christy and Lucy's mum.

"That must be what Miss Louisa meant," Lucy's mum murmured. "I wonder what they're here for."

"Maybe they need dancers for a show. Or perhaps they're going to be in a film!" Ellie whispered, her eyes wide. "Lucy told us that Miss Louisa sometimes finds performers for TV and films."

Lucy's mum smiled at her. "That would be great, wouldn't it? Oh, shush a minute. I think Miss Louisa's giving us a look."

At the end of the class, the woman who'd been watching got up and came to talk to Miss Louisa. She was nodding, and Miss Louisa looked pleased.

"Remember I mentioned a surprise? This is Carla from Eclipse Productions, girls," Miss Louisa announced. "They're about to film a TV commercial close by, and Carla wants to ask some of you to audition for them."

A thrilled whisper ran through the class, and Ellie beamed triumphantly at Christy and Lucy's mum. She'd been right. She crossed all her fingers, hoping that they would pick Lucy for the audition.

Carla had a quick conversation with Miss Louisa, pointing to different girls, and then Miss Louisa called Lucy and two others to stay behind. Everyone else trailed out to get changed, looking rather disappointed.

Carla had a chat with Lucy and the other two girls, and gave them some paperwork. Then Lucy came running over to Ellie and Christy and her mum, looking really happy. "Did you hear, Mum? An audition! It's next Saturday, can I go?"

Her mum was reading the letter on the top of the sheaf of papers. "I suppose so, Lucy. It says the filming would only take one day, oh, and it's in half-term, so you wouldn't miss school." She laughed. "Why not? But remember, Lucy, there might be lots of people auditioning. Don't get too excited yet, will you?"

Lucy shook her head, but Ellie could see that her eyes were sparkling. Of course she was excited! Ellie was excited too, and she was only a friend of the person going to an audition.

"Come on then." Lucy's mum led them out of the studio. "Let's go to the DVD shop and choose a film to watch. And we'll have a proper read of all this at home."

The girls were so desperate to get back and read all about Lucy's audition that they chose a DVD in about two minutes, without any arguing.

"I wonder what the ad is for?" Christy asked, as they walked back to Lucy's house.

"I'm sure it'll say somewhere in all that stuff." Lucy's mum glanced at the papers sticking out of her handbag. "I hope it's not for something you hate, Lucy. Like eggs!"

Lucy made a face. "I don't think I could

eat an egg, even if I was going to be on TV," she agreed. "But I'd definitely try!" she added. "I can't believe I'm going to an audition."

When they got home, Lucy's mum spread out the papers over the kitchen table, and everyone squished up next to her to look.

"So the audition's at the production company's office. Oh, and we need to apply for a licence, if you get the part," Lucy's mum murmured. "I hadn't realized it was all so complicated."

Lucy was scanning the different bits of paper, trying to find out what she might have to do. "It must say somewhere," she muttered. "Ooh, if it's for a clothes shop I might get to keep some!"

Ellie laughed, as she held up the piece of paper she'd been reading. "I'm not sure you'll want to keep anything from this advert, Lucy. You could pass it on to me or Christy though."

"What is it? Tell me!" Lucy asked excitedly.

"Dog food!"

Chapter Three

The Horrible Howler

"Barkers dog food... Ohh." Lucy read the description of the ad. "Do you think there'll be a dog in it? I'll have to act with a dog?"

"I don't think there's a dog at the audition, not from what it says here," her mum put in. "But I imagine there'll be a dog in the actual ad. Are you sure you want to do this, Lucy?"

Lucy nibbled her bottom lip, looking worried. Then at last she nodded. "I might never get another chance. And it isn't as if

I'll get the part anyway! I just want to see what it's like going to an audition."

Her mum frowned, looking concerned. "You never know. They picked you and Tasha and Sam out of the class, they obviously thought you were good."

"That lady - Carla - she said you had stage presence," Ellie added.

Lucy hugged her mum. "It'll be fine, Mum. If I get the part - which I won't - then I'll just have to be brave, won't I?"

"I bet a dog that does acting would be really well-trained," Ellie said. "It would be too nicely behaved to scare you." She gave a tiny sigh. It would be lovely if Rascal was like that. He'd accidentally upset Lucy the first time she'd met him, even though her friend loved him now.

Christy was nodding. "You really like Rascal and Bouncer, don't you? Bouncer's a big dog, as well. And Rascal's ... well, he's bouncy... I'm sure you'd be OK. And you shouldn't go to the audition thinking you won't get it. You have to think you're a star!"

Lucy blushed pink. "I've never really done any acting, though. I'm a dancer."

Ellie suddenly sat up, beaming. "I've got a brilliant idea. Dogs can tell when you're nervous, it makes them really play up sometimes. We just have to get rid of your nerves! The audition's on Saturday, so that gives us a whole week to get you really happy with dogs. Then if they ask you at the audition whether you like them, you won't even have to pretend. Would it be all right if Lucy came to the park with me and Christy and our dogs a couple of times this week?" she asked Lucy's mum.

"Sounds like a great idea. But now we need to think about tea, otherwise you'll never get to watch that film." Lucy's mum got up quickly, and then groaned as the phone rang. "Hello? Oh! Ellie, it's your mum."

Ellie took the phone, looking surprised. "Hi, Mum. Is everything OK?"

"Hello, Ellie. I'm having a bit of a problem with Rascal, I'm afraid."

"What's the matter with him?" Ellie asked anxiously. "He's not ill, is he?"

"No, he's absolutely fine, don't panic. He's just being difficult." Ellie's mum sounded stressed, and Ellie realized that the funny noise in the background was Rascal. He was howling very, very loudly.

"I can hear him, Mum! He sounds really upset." Ellie gripped the phone tightly. It was hard to listen to Rascal sounding so miserable. Maybe she should go home.

"You were right, Ellie. He doesn't like you not being here and he's making a fuss," said Mum. "But he has to get used to it, or you'll never be able to go anywhere!"

"I suppose so..." Ellie murmured.

"Anyway, I rang up so you can talk to him. Tell him to be quiet, Ellie, please! I'll hold the phone up to him."

"Is that Rascal?" Christy whispered. "Is he missing you?"

Ellie nodded. Then there was a curious snuffling sound on the other end of the phone, and Ellie giggled. Even though she was worried about Rascal,

it was funny to think of him on the phone to her. "Hey, Rascal..."

There was an excited little yap at the end of the line, and she heard her mum's voice, sounding a bit distant. "Keep talking to him, Ellie. Thank goodness he's stopped making that awful noise."

"It's OK, Rascal. I'll be back home tomorrow. I'll see you really soon, I promise. Did you go for a walk? Did Mum give you your tea?"

"That was the only time he did stop howling," her mother muttered. "He's looking a lot less upset now, Ellie. Hopefully he understands that you'll be coming back tomorrow. Have a lovely time at Lucy's, and tell her mum I'm sorry I had to disturb you all. We'll see you tomorrow, OK? Have fun!"

"Bye, Mum!" Ellie ended the call, and gave the phone back to Lucy's mum. Poor Rascal. Maybe he really had thought that she'd left him for ever. The only other time he'd seen her pack a big bag was to go to Gran's, but that time they'd taken him too.

"Was he missing you?" Lucy asked.

"Yes, he was driving Mum mad. But he's OK now." Ellie crossed her fingers. She wondered if Rascal would sleep in his basket for once, or if he'd go and sleep on Max's bed. She didn't think Lila would have him.

Ellie gave a little sigh. She'd been fine till Mum called. But now she really missed Rascal too!

After the excitement of the audition news, the girls found it really hard to settle down to watching the film in their sleeping bags. Then they talked in whispers late into the night – until Lucy's mum came down to check on them and told them to go to sleep.

The next morning, they spread out the pet magazines all over the living-room floor, and tried to work out the best possible pet for Lucy.

"I'd really like a mouse," she said thoughtfully. "I love them being so tiny. But Mum's not keen at all. She says their tails look like worms."

Ellie wrinkled her nose. "I can see what

your mum means," she admitted.

Christy nodded, and then squeaked excitedly. "I know! Pass me that one." She grabbed the magazine Lucy was holding. "Look, I knew there was something in here." She showed Lucy a picture of a soft, golden-brown creature, with big black

eyes. And a lovely long, furry tail. "Gerbils! They look a bit like mice, but they've got furry tails!"

"Oh, he's so cute..." Lucy stroked the photo. "I never thought of a gerbil."

Christy smiled proudly. "Your mum couldn't not like him, could she?"

Chapter Four

Amazing News!

When Ellie got home, Rascal was so excited to see her that she thought he might burst from barking. And since then he'd insisted on following her everywhere. If she went to the loo, he sat outside the door making worried noises, as though he thought she might climb out of the bathroom window and leave him.

They were having Grandad, Auntie Gemma and Liam over for Sunday lunch, and every time Ellie went to open the front

door, Rascal was glued to her heels.

"Hello, Ellie!" Grandad gave her a hug. "How was your sleepover?"

"It was great! Lucy's got an audition to be in a dog-food ad! And she thinks she might get a pet gerbil. But Rascal was really missing me, Grandad. Mum had to ring up so I could talk to him, because he wouldn't stop howling."

Rascal looked up at Grandad. He was sitting by Ellie's feet, with a saintly expression on his face. *Who, me?* he seemed to be saying.

"Little monster." Grandad rubbed Rascal's ears. "You've got them all wrapped around your tiny paw, haven't you? Are Liam and Gemma here yet, Ellie?"

"Yes, they're in the kitchen with Mum and Dad." Ellie and Grandad went through to the kitchen, where Mum was preparing the roast lunch.

Auntie Gemma was looking very smart, in a bright pink dress. When Ellie came in, she glanced up at her boyfriend Liam, and then smiled at Ellie. "Could you get Max and Lila to come down, Ellie? I've got some news, and I can't wait any longer!"

Ellie dashed upstairs to yell for Max and Lila, and soon everyone was squashed round the kitchen table.

"We're getting married!" Auntie Gemma announced. She waved her hand around, showing a sparkly engagement ring, with a green stone in it.

"Let me see, let me see!" demanded Lila, grabbing Auntie Gemma's hand. "Oohhh, it's gorgeous!"

"It's an emerald. I've had my hand in my dress pocket ever since we got here, I wanted to tell you all at once!"

"Oh, Gemma, that's great news." Ellie's mum was almost crying. "When are you getting married? Soon?"

Liam nodded. "Very soon. This spring! Gemma's started making plans already."

"I knew it!" Ellie told Auntie Gemma. "When you found the ring in the Christmas pudding!"

Auntie Gemma smiled. "I'm sure that did help Liam think it was the right time. Will you and Lila be my bridesmaids, Ellie?"

Ellie beamed, and Lila hugged Auntie Gemma. "What are you going to wear? What do you want us to wear? Hang on, I saw the most amazing wedding dress in a magazine, I've got it upstairs somewhere."

Mum laughed. "Lila's going to be your wedding planner if you're not careful, Gemma. Oh, goodness, I nearly forgot about lunch! Max, Ellie, can you help me bring all the dishes over?"

Ellie got up, and sighed as Rascal immediately jumped out of his bed, and sidled up next to her leg, in case she might be about to leave him again.

Lila raced back into the kitchen, waving her magazine, which had photos of a singer's wedding. "Look at this! Isn't it the nicest dress? I don't really like her music, but that doesn't matter."

"As long as we don't have to play any of her songs at the wedding." Liam shuddered.

Ellie hurried over to the table, clutching a big dish of peas, eager to see the dress.

Or rather, she meant to hurry to the table. She forgot about Rascal, attached to her feet, and tripped over him, sending the bowl flying and an avalanche of peas all over the floor and the table. And Lila's magazine.

"Are you OK, Ellie?" Mum asked, helping her up.

Ellie nodded. "Did I squash Rascal?" she asked in an anxious voice, looking around for him.

"No," Mum sighed. "He's under the table, eating the peas..."

Dad was looking at the photos in the magazine, which were now mostly green. "I think a green wedding dress would suit you, Gemma. It's a bit different, anyway..."

Auntie Gemma didn't look as though she thought it was very funny.

"And that's what it's been like ever since!" Ellie told Christy and Lucy at school the next morning. "Wedding, wedding, wedding! I'm really excited about being a bridesmaid, but Mum and Auntie Gemma couldn't talk about anything else. And Lila's just as bad." She shook her head. "I'm glad to get away from them all to go to the park with the dogs this afternoon. You're both still OK to come, aren't you? We can't go for too long, because I've got dog training, but even a little bit of practice will help."

They had arranged that Lucy and Ellie would come over to Christy's, and Christy's mum would take the three girls and Rascal and Bouncer to the park, so they could try to thoroughly de-scare Lucy.

"What are you going to do, exactly?" Lucy asked, looking a little nervous.

"We're not telling you," Christy said firmly. "But it's nothing you need to be worried about, we promise."

Ellie nodded. She had given Rascal a firm talking-to that morning, all about how he had to be on his best behaviour, and not scare Lucy. He'd stared at her, his big brown eyes looking very innocent, and she'd been absolutely sure he was listening. But then he'd given her a massive lick all down her nose. So maybe not.

"First, you have to lie down." Ellie pointed dramatically at the grass, and Lucy looked horrified.

"Why? It's all muddy!"

"It isn't *that* muddy," Ellie argued, looking around the park. "Oh, OK. Maybe it is. Please can you lie on this bench then?"

"I'm not sure about this," Lucy muttered, but she did as she was told, peering nervously sideways to try and see what Ellie and Christy and the dogs were doing.

"What's that?" she gasped, when Ellie scattered something over her coat. "What are you doing, Ellie?"

"It's OK," Christy said soothingly. "It's dog treats, that's all. We've covered you in dog treats, and Rascal and Bouncer are going to eat them off you. They'll be really gentle, I promise. You won't even feel them, probably."

Lucy didn't actually fling herself off the bench, but she looked like she wanted to. They'd already made her hold the dogs' leads and run up and down the park, and got her to play Frisbee with them, but this was a bit different.

Bouncer started delicately crunching the dog treats off Lucy's knees, and she giggled. "It's all tickly!"

"See? We told you it would be all right," Ellie said. "You're going to be fine on Saturday after this. We can do a last-minute top-up session on Saturday morning before the audition, too."

Rascal was standing on his hind legs, trying to join in with Bouncer, but the bench was too tall for him.

"Oh no, I didn't think about Rascal not being able to reach," Ellie muttered. "Maybe if you hold your arm out, Lucy. Rascal, no!"

Rascal had given up waiting. The smell of all those dog treats was just too good, and he simply went for them. He jumped on to the bench, straight on to Lucy's tummy, and starting wolfing down every treat he could see. He had some catching up to do.

Bouncer obviously decided that if Rascal was jumping up, he could too. He planted his hefty front paws right on to Lucy's knees, ignoring her squeaks, and went on hoovering up the treats.

Lucy was giggling and gasping, "Get them off me! I'm squashed!" while Ellie and Christy tried to remove the dogs. But

Rascal wasn't letting anyone catch him when there were still loads of his favourite treats everywhere.

Once the dogs had finished off all the treats, Christy and Ellie put them back on their leads, and joined Lucy on the bench.

"That was really funny!" said Lucy, still wheezing with laughter. "How can Rascal be so heavy? He's tiny!"

Ellie hugged her. "You've just had two dogs jumping all over you, Lucy! And you're laughing about it!"

Lucy stared at her. "Did you do that on purpose?" she demanded.

"No," Ellie admitted. "It went a bit wrong. We never meant for them to jump on you. But it's worked, hasn't it? You weren't scared?"

Lucy shook her head, smiling. "I was laughing too much," she admitted.

"There you are then," Christy said. "Mission accomplished!"

Lucy frowned. "But I want to know exactly what you're planning for the final session before the audition on Saturday!"

Chapter Five

The Biggest Dog in the World

It was Saturday morning, and Christy and Ellie were in Ellie's living room. They were waiting for Lucy's mum to bring her round for a last quick de-scaring session before her audition. The girls still weren't sure exactly what they were going to do. Lucy's mum wasn't as used to dogs as Christy's mum was, and Ellie didn't think she'd be happy about Rascal and Bouncer jumping all over Lucy.

"What about the same thing again?" Christy suggested. "It worked last time!"

Ellie shook her head. "I'm not sure... Oh, there's the door!"

She came back with Lucy following her, and looking rather worried.

"How are you feeling?" Ellie asked.

Lucy sighed. "I'm so nervous about this audition – I'm just going to look stupid."

She did look really pale, and sort of trembly, Ellie realized. "Hey, you mustn't worry. Come and sit down." She towed Lucy over to sit next to Christy, who was on the floor. She was leaning against the sofa, with Bouncer's head in her lap. Ellie sat down next to them, and Rascal immediately curled up on her legs, and rested his nose on Lucy's knees, looking up at her and wagging his tail. "See, he wants to cheer you up!"

Lucy giggled and patted Rascal's head. Then she laughed out loud as Bouncer heaved himself more on top of Christy, so that his nose was close enough for Lucy to stroke too.

"Ooof, Bouncer, you're too big for that," Christy groaned.

Ellie watched thoughtfully as Lucy stroked both dogs, and they nuzzled her back. Lucy looked a bit less nervous already.

So maybe not having a plan had worked out for the best after all...

"I wish she'd ring and tell us how it went..." Ellie moaned, staring at the phone. "The audition was at eleven, it must have finished by now."

"It's only half-past," Mum pointed out. "They're probably just setting off home."

"I suppose," Ellie sighed. She looked over at Rascal, snoozing in his basket.

He'd been fantastic at cheering Lucy up that morning. Ellie was sure that Lucy could have told the people at the audition quite truthfully that she liked dogs.

The phone rang, and even though Ellie had been staring at it, waiting for it to ring, it made her jump. She grabbed it out of the holder, her fingers fumbling for the answer button. "Hello?"

"I got the part!" It was Lucy, squealing with delight. "They said I was great, and they wouldn't usually say straight away, but they thought I was just right!"

"That's brilliant! Well done!" Ellie beamed at her mum, making a thumbs-up sign.

"We're just in the car now – Mum let me use her mobile," Lucy explained.

"So was there a dog?" Ellie asked. She knew Lucy had hoped there wouldn't be.

"No..." Lucy sounded worried.

"What's the matter?"

"They showed me a picture of the dog. He's really big, Ellie. Really, really big. Bigger than Bouncer, I think. And he's still only a puppy, it's a commercial for food for growing dogs. But I can't imagine that one growing any bigger!"

"Wow." Ellie could see why Lucy was worried. "Oh! You met Hugo at the Christmas Fair, didn't you? Remember the enormous Great Dane? Was he like that?"

"Kind of," Lucy agreed. "Yes, he might

be one of those. I'm not sure I can cope with a dog that big. The script says I've got to do tricks with him! How am I supposed to do that?"

Ellie's mind was whirring. "OK. Look, the filming isn't until half-term. We've got a bit of time. I'll see if I can get Jack and Hugo to join in our de-scaring course. I bet Jack would help. And Hugo's lovely, he's a big softie, I promise. Don't worry, Lucy! We'll sort it out."

It was Thursday night, and Ellie and Lucy were in the little park close to the village hall where Jo held their dog-training classes. Lucy's mum was sitting on one of the benches, chatting to Jack's mum and Ellie's dad.

Lucy only had a few more days until the filming of her TV ad, on the Monday of half-term. She'd been getting more and more worried about the dog in the photo all that week, and she'd been asking Ellie every day if she'd arranged for her to meet Hugo, but tonight was the first chance they'd had.

"Why do you have to take the dogs for a walk before dog training?" Lucy asked, looking confused.

"It wears them out a bit," Jack explained. "That way, they're better at doing what they're told." He grinned. "Hugo needs all the help he can get."

"And it means they can have a wee before they go into the hall," Ellie pointed out. "Rascal weed up one of the radiators once," she admitted. "It was so embarrassing."

Jack shuddered. "Hugo's never done that. Yet."

Ellie giggled. "He might flood the hall if he did!"

"Can I stroke him?" Lucy asked Jack suddenly. She'd been working herself up to do it, Ellie realized.

"Course. He's very friendly," Jack promised her. "He likes being scratched under the chin and behind his ears."

Cautiously, Lucy reached out her hand and rubbed Hugo's soft ears, as lightly as she possibly could.

Hugo looked rather surprised, and his ears twitched as though he thought maybe a fly had landed on him.

"More than that!" Ellie told her.

Nodding, Lucy patted Hugo's ears a little more firmly, and he closed his eyes and wagged his tail.

"See how friendly he is," Ellie pointed out. "Just because he's big it doesn't mean he's fierce or anything."

Jack shook his head. "He's never hurt anybody. Well, except me, and that's only because he tries to sit on me."

Lucy smiled. She'd stopped looking quite so nervous, and she even laughed as she watched Rascal and Hugo chasing round the park after each other, to work off some energy before the class.

"Ugh, there's Amelia, and Goldie," Ellie muttered, nodding at a girl who'd been at their school till that year, and her perfect little spaniel.

"I keep hoping she's going to move up a class," Jack said gloomily. "But no such luck."

"Come on, Rascal! It's time for dog training," Ellie called, and Jack waved Hugo's lead at him hopefully.

"He really isn't scary," Lucy said to Jack and Ellie, as she watched Hugo doing his party trick, drinking out of a bottle of water that Jack held up to the side of his mouth.

"See? I told you so!" Ellie said triumphantly. "Now you can go to your film shoot and not worry about that big dog. Everything will be fine."

Ellie and Jack waved goodbye to Lucy, and dashed off to their class.

"Wow, look at all these extra dogs!" Jack muttered, as they came into the hall.

Several new owners were standing at the side of the hall, most of them looking a bit nervous. One girl about their age had a Dalmatian puppy, and she looked so worried, she reminded Ellie of how *she* used to feel at dog training. *I don't worry about it so much now,* Ellie thought to herself with surprise. *Rascal must have got better!*

Jo stepped into the middle of the hall to start the class. "Hello, everyone. As you can see, we're pretty full today. Which means I'd like some of you with slightly older dogs to move up to the intermediate class after half-term."

Ellie saw Amelia looking smug, and sighed. Amelia and Goldie were bound to move up. Goldie always did as she was told.

"Did you hear that?" Jack hissed.

Ellie blinked. She hadn't really been listening as Jo read out the names. "What?"

"We're moving up! Rascal and Hugo!"

"Really? Wow!" Ellie beamed proudly. "Well done, Rascal!"

Rascal just yawned, but Ellie didn't mind. He was an intermediate dog now!

Chapter Six
Dog Disaster

"Oh, why does the phone always ring when I'm cooking!" Mum sighed, and licked her buttery fingers before she picked it up. "And watch Rascal, Ellie, he's about to go for that bit of pastry!" She shook her head. "If Jo could see him at home, I bet she wouldn't be putting him up to the intermediate class!"

Ellie swiped the pastry out of the way, and giggled as Rascal glared at her. That pastry had been his!

"It's Lucy, for you." Mum sounded surprised. She handed Ellie the phone, and Ellie heard Lucy's panicky voice on the other end of the line. She gave Mum a worried look. It was Monday, the day of the shoot for the ad, and Ellie had been sure that Lucy would be fine! What could have gone wrong? Lucy had popped round the afternoon before to borrow Rascal to rehearse the script with, and it had gone brilliantly. Lucy had been looking forward to the shoot – Ellie would never have believed that she used to be afraid of dogs. She'd known all her lines perfectly too.

In the ad, Lucy was supposed to throw a ball for her dog to fetch, and she had Rascal racing up and down the garden so many times that he gave up in the end, and went and hid under a bush to sulk because he was too worn out.

So what had gone wrong?

"What's the matter?" Ellie asked Lucy anxiously. "Is it the dog?"

"Yes!" Lucy wailed. "He's called Freddie and he's huge! Well, actually he's not as big as Hugo, but he's not friendly like Hugo is, so he seems bigger. He's really, really scary!"

Ellie didn't know what to say. She'd been so sure that Lucy would be OK.

"He jumped up at me when I was supposed to throw the ball for him," Lucy explained, sounding rather tearful. "I really thought he was going to bite me. The lady who owns him said he just wanted the ball, but his teeth were so near my hand. I don't think I'm being stupid, Ellie, he's not a nice dog like Rascal or Bouncer or Hugo."

"So what happened after he jumped at you?" Ellie asked.

Lucy sighed. "I fell over. And my costume got all muddy, so now everyone's annoyed because they had to sponge it clean, and it took ages. Then we tried again, and Freddie growled at me, and I forgot my lines." She really was crying now. "I'm going to lose the part, I'm sure I am."

"Why can't they get a different dog?" Ellie said crossly. It didn't seem fair on Lucy at all.

"They are trying, but it's hard to find a dog at the last minute," Lucy explained. "Ellie, can I ask you a huge, huge favour? Would you come over to the set? It isn't far from your house at all. They said they might let me keep the part if I can do it with a different dog... I told them I knew a really sweet, clever dog, and he's very funny, and I'm not scared of him... And he's the right age – still a puppy, but an older puppy..."

It took Ellie a few seconds to realize what Lucy meant – that the funny, clever dog she was talking about was Rascal.

"You want Rascal to be in the ad with you?" Ellie squeaked delightedly.

"Yes! He is sweet, Ellie, you know he is. I bet they'd love him. The director said Jack Russells were cute. And I'm not scared of Rascal at all any more. I'm sure I could do the ad with him."

Ellie nodded, and then remembered that she was on the phone and Lucy couldn't see her. "Do you think he'd be able to do it?" she asked Lucy. "What about the rolling?"

The dog in the ad had to roll over, and Ellie had thought that sounded great in the script. She'd asked Jo how you trained a dog to roll over, at the end of their class on Thursday. It was a difficult one to do, Jo had explained, because most dogs don't like to show off their tummies. It was the way a dog would signal that he thought he had lost a fight, and he wanted to give in.

Rascal didn't seem to mind showing his tummy, but it was still tricky. It had taken them a while to go through the moves, as the dogs had to start off with "down", which they already knew, and then learn to roll on to their side, their back and finally the right way up again. Rascal had sort of managed it when Lucy practised with him on Sunday, but Ellie wasn't sure he could do it on command.

Lucy sighed. "He might be able to. He was great at fetching when we practised, wasn't he? I know he's naughty sometimes, but that Freddie wouldn't do what he was told either. His owner tried to stop him jumping up at me and he wouldn't. She said it was because he could tell I was scared."

Ellie frowned thoughtfully. "All right. I'm going to ask Mum. Lila's gone shopping and Max is over at Lewis's house, so we were just doing some cooking. I bet she won't mind."

Ellie smiled up at her mum, who was looking at her curiously. "Actually, she'll probably love coming to a film set! Get your mum to tell her where we need to go!" Ellie thrust the phone at her mum, and picked Rascal up. "Would you like to be a TV star, Rascal?" she asked him, dancing around.

Rascal gave a loud yap.

Ellie was pretty sure that meant "yes"!

Chapter Seven

A Starring Role!

"Wait for me, Ellie!" Mum was hurrying along after them, as Ellie read the house numbers, and Rascal bounced excitedly on the end of his lead, sensing that something special was happening.

"It must be soon," Ellie called back. "This is number fifty, and we're looking for seventy-three." She looked down the street, frowning. It didn't seem at all smart enough to be used as a film set. But the lady at the

audition had told Lucy that it was used a lot, as it had a beautiful garden. It had been in loads of TV programmes, apparently, when they wanted a "normal" sort of house.

"Look, here it is." Ellie hung back suddenly, feeling shy. The front door of number seventy-three was open, and a man was carrying some equipment in from one of the big vans parked outside. There was a catering van too. People were hurrying around inside the house, looking busy, and Ellie didn't like to disturb them. Then a black-haired lady carrying a clipboard spotted her, and came over, looking hopeful. "Are you Lucy's friend? The one with the puppy? Is this him?"

73

Ellie nodded, and realized it was Carla, the same lady from the dance class. "This is Rascal," she explained. "Lucy called me..."

"Yes, it's been a disaster!" Carla rolled her eyes. "That Freddie was supposed to be really sweet-natured, but he didn't get on with Lucy at all and we had to send him home." She looked down at Rascal worriedly. "He's very small..."

"He's a Jack Russell!" Ellie said firmly. "He's just the right size."

"OK. Well, let's see if Dan likes him."

Ellie had no idea who Dan was, but she and Mum followed Carla through the house out into the garden, which was a tangle of cables, growing enormous lights instead of flowers. It was a truly weird-looking place.

If Ellie glanced at it sideways, it almost seemed like a normal garden, but then she could see that half the plants were artificial, or real ones that must have been brought over in pots to make it look like summertime.

Lucy was sitting on a folding chair to one side, looking anxious. She was wearing a pretty summer dress, with her coat on over the top. Her mum was beside her, and she nudged Lucy when she saw Ellie and Rascal coming.

"Oh, thank you, Ellie!" Lucy dashed over to hug her. "You're such a star. And you're going to be a star too, Rascal."

Lucy took Ellie's hand and pulled her over to a huddle of people looking at something on a laptop.

Carla followed them. "Dan, this is the new dog," she called.

A tall, very thin man with a worried face and huge eyebrows turned round to look at them all. His eyebrows flew up when he caught sight of Rascal, but then he walked round Ellie and Rascal thoughtfully.

Rascal sat down and panted up at him, his tongue hanging out cheerfully.

"He might be all right," Dan muttered, crouching down and staring at Rascal. "I had a much bigger dog in mind, of course, but still..."

Rascal barked at him and wagged his tail, and Dan laughed. "He's certainly a little character. Heard me saying you ought to be bigger, did you?" He glanced up at Ellie. "Can he do tricks? Does he fetch, roll over, that kind of thing?"

"Some tricks..." Ellie said slowly. Rascal did fetch. She still wasn't quite so sure about the rolling over. But she wasn't going to say that.

"Well, we'll give it a go. Can you just wait over there for the minute? We'll get everything set up again. Lucy said you'd seen the script? You know what he has to do?"

Ellie nodded. She just hoped Rascal would do as he was told. She and Mum hurried over to sit next to Lucy, who looked frozen in her summer dress. Lucy's mum took Ellie's to go and get a cup of tea, and the girls and Rascal were alone for a moment.

"I think Dan likes Rascal!" Ellie told Lucy. "Show me the script again."

Lucy handed it to her, and Ellie read it

through carefully. Rascal ought to be able to do it all. It started with Lucy laughing at him as he rolled over and over.

"We might need more dog treats," Ellie muttered.

"Ugh! Get it off me!"

Ellie and Lucy looked up at once. They'd been peering at the script, and Ellie hadn't noticed that Rascal was at the end of his lead, exploring. Now he was gazing up at a woman who'd been sitting on a chair close to them. She was staring down at her foot with a disgusted expression on her face.

"Oh! She's playing my mum," Lucy whispered. "I don't think she likes dogs very much."

"It licked me!" the woman told Ellie frostily. She was wearing pretty summer sandals, and there was a lot of foot on show for Rascal to lick.

"I'm really sorry," Ellie apologized, even though she didn't feel like it. She scooped Rascal up. It was only a little bit of lick! And Rascal was a "he", not an "it"!

Chapter Eight

Going Barkers

It looked like the actress wanted to make even more of a fuss, but a young man with spiky hair came over just then, and introduced himself as Ben, the dog wrangler. Ellie wasn't quite sure that she wanted Rascal wrangled, but apparently Ben was just supposed to make Rascal do the stuff that was needed for the filming. He started off by trying to give him a wash and brush-up, which didn't go well. Rascal didn't see why his claws needed polishing, and he kept wriggling out of Ben's grip.

The filming wasn't nearly as exciting as Ellie had thought it would be. There seemed to be endless stops and starts, as the crew tinkered with lights and moved screens here and there to reflect the artificial sunlight around.

Rascal was bored too. After Ellie had stopped him exploring the garden, he had to sit and wait by the chairs, and every so often he was taken to stand under hot lights. He didn't have any idea why, and he didn't like them very much.

"OK, let's start filming the rolling-over sequence." Dan beckoned to Ben, Ellie and Rascal to come and join Lucy under the lights. "We want him to roll over and over, and then leap up. Right?"

Ellie nodded, but she was panicking inside. She really wasn't sure if Rascal could do that, especially when the instructions were coming from Ben and not her. But she didn't want to say so in case they decided to get Freddie the "trained" dog back, and to take Lucy's part away from her.

She watched anxiously as Ben said, "Down, Rascal! Roll over!"

Rascal simply put his head on one side and stared at Ben curiously.

The film crew laughed. He was very cute, with his head on one side like that, looking at Ben as if he thought the man was rather strange.

"Shall I try?" Ellie asked nervously. "He's not used to other people telling him what to do..."

Ben looked slightly annoyed, but he nodded, and Ellie grabbed the treats she'd brought with her. "Down! Roll over, Rascal!" She rattled the bag of dog treats temptingly, and Rascal eyed it.

"Roll over!" Ellie tried to make her voice as encouraging as possible, and Rascal seemed to suddenly remember what he was supposed to do. He lay down, and then flipped over on to his back, waving all four paws in the air, and wagging his tail at the same time.

"Good boy!" Ellie told him, wishing she could get a bit closer. But she couldn't be in the shot with Rascal. "Roll over. Roll over."

Rascal did it twice more, as she'd asked, and then he got up, and marched out of shot and determinedly over to Ellie, as if he'd given up waiting, and he'd like his treats now, thank you very much.

Ellie gave him several out of the packet, and looked up hopefully at Dan. Had that been what they wanted?

Dan was frowning at the laptop where they were playing back the last shot. "I'm still not totally happy with the light," he mused. "Oh, and can he do it faster, please?"

Ellie shook her head. There was really no point pretending. "I'm sorry, it's not his best trick. I don't think he can go any faster."

Dan sighed. "Well, we'll do another take, and see if we can improve the light anyway."

Eventually, Dan was happy with the shots of Rascal rolling over, and they moved on to Lucy's "mum" putting down a bowl of delicious Barkers food. She cooed delightedly at Rascal while she did it, as though she thought he was gorgeous. Ellie was impressed – she was obviously a very good actress.

Rascal was supposed to wolf the food down eagerly, and this was the one part of the ad that Ellie hadn't worried about. Rascal ate everything, all the time. Even things that weren't food.

So when the actress put down the big bowl of Barkers, Ellie wasn't expecting Rascal to look thoughtfully at it, and then lie down as though he were planning a nap.

Everyone was rather surprised, and they did it all over again.

Rascal walked off set, looking bored.

"Yummy food, Rascal!" Ellie hissed. It was no good. She didn't know if Rascal just wasn't hungry after all the dog treats, but there was no way he was going to eat the dog food.

Ellie giggled nervously as he did it a third time. It was quite funny that the whole ad was meant to show how delicious Barkers was for growing dogs, and Rascal clearly didn't like it at all! "Um, I don't think he likes it," she told Dan apologetically.

"This is ridiculous!" snapped a man in a suit, who'd been standing behind the lights, watching. "That's our extra-meaty kind.

It's very popular. Dogs love it! They go barkers for it! That's our slogan!"

Ellie opened her mouth, and then shut it again quickly. She hadn't realized that someone from the dog-food company was watching.

"Ellie!" Lucy whispered. She was looking a bit green. The smell of Barkers was very strong. "I've got an idea..."

Five minutes later, Ellie smiled at Dan, and the dog-food man, with her fingers crossed behind her back. "I'm sure he'll be fine now," she explained. "He, er, just needed a wee. That's all."

Dan gave her a slightly doubtful look, but he called everyone back for another take.

Ellie watched hopefully as the actress put down the bowl of food for Rascal. The girls had begged the caterers for ham sandwiches, then they'd taken out all the ham and hidden it under the Barkers while everyone was gathered round muttering about the lighting again. As a final touch, Lucy had rubbed ham all over the outside of the bowl, so that it would smell yummy to Rascal.

"Look at that!" the dog-food man said triumphantly, as soon as they'd finished the shot. "Wolfing it down! I told you dogs love it."

Ellie smiled, hoping he wouldn't spot Rascal tugging the bits of ham out from underneath the dog food...

Chapter Nine

Making a Splash

Rascal's final scene was the one they'd spent ages practising the day before. Lucy was confident throwing a ball for him to fetch now, and firm enough to take it out of his mouth when he brought it back to her. Sometimes he liked to hang on to it, and growl a little bit. But Ellie was sure that Lucy wouldn't mind that after their practice.

Rascal had had a bit of a rest while all the equipment was moved around for the new shot, and he was feeling bright and bouncy and full of ham. He barked delightedly when he saw the ball in Lucy's hand, and there were admiring murmurs from the crew as he skipped and danced around Lucy, looking like the happiest dog ever. Exactly what they needed for the shot. Ellie smiled proudly. Finally he was behaving himself!

Lucy wasn't meant to throw the ball very far, as there wasn't a huge lot of space in the garden and they needed to be able to keep Rascal in the shot as he fetched it.

The first couple of throws went too wide. Rascal happily fetched them anyway, but Dan was shaking his head.

"Try moving back a bit," he called to Lucy. "Mind the pond though!"

The best part of the garden, Ellie thought, was the big fish pond in the middle. It had amazing fat koi carp swimming in it, which luckily Rascal hadn't noticed or they wouldn't have been able to get him to do anything.

Lucy edged backwards carefully.

"Lovely. Nice view of the pond behind." Dan nodded happily, and Lucy tried again.

It was a perfect throw. Too perfect, actually. Lucy lobbed the ball gently towards Rascal, in exactly the right place, just in front of him. Rascal gave a huge leap into the air, seized the ball in his teeth – and hurtled towards Lucy's arms, scrabbling his paws and expecting her to catch him, just like Ellie usually did.

But Lucy didn't catch him. Ellie watched in horror as Rascal landed at her feet, and Lucy toppled over backwards, straight into the lily pond.

Ellie ran to help the crew fish her out, hoping that she wasn't hurt. What if she'd hit her head? But Lucy was fine – just wet and cold. Everyone crowded round her, fetching towels and fussing, and then she was hurried into the house to get dry.

Ellie looked round at Dan, thinking she should go and apologize, but then she realized he was laughing. He was holding Rascal, who was licking his ear happily.

There was a laptop set up, and Dan was watching the footage of Lucy falling in the pond, and he looked delighted.

The man from the dog-food company was nodding. "Really funny. Just the impression we want. Loads of energy, and all because of Barkers dog food."

"Perfect. We're all done then." Dan tickled Rascal's ears. "You turned out to be a little star, didn't you?"

Ellie hid her smile. She wasn't going to tell them it was actually all down to ham.

She took Rascal back from Dan, and hurried indoors to see how Lucy was.

"I'm really sorry!" she whispered to Lucy, who was wrapped up in a huge fleecy robe and was sitting with her mum, drinking a mug of hot chocolate. "Are you OK?"

Lucy nodded, but she looked worried. "Are they really cross?" she asked.

Ellie shook her head. "No! They think it's fantastic, and they want to put it in the ad." She gazed doubtfully at Lucy. Would she mind being on TV falling in a pond?

But Lucy didn't seem to mind at all. "They do?" she asked happily. "Oh, Ellie, that's brilliant. I thought they were going to get rid of me!" She kissed the top of Rascal's head. "You're such a star!"

Chapter Ten

Dog Star!

"That's such a lot of money!" Christy sounded very impressed.

Lucy smiled, looking embarrassed and a bit proud of herself. "I did have to fall in a pond for it," she pointed out. "Anyway, Mum says most of it has to go in my savings account, but I'm allowed to go to Pet Life and buy my gerbils and all their stuff!"

It was three weeks after they'd filmed the dog-food ad, and Lucy had been sent a cheque in the post. Her mum had phoned Ellie's mum and Christy's, to ask if the girls could go to the pet shop after school.

"I love Pet Life," Ellie said happily, as they climbed into Lucy's mum's car. "Mum wouldn't give me an advance on my pocket money though. She says Rascal doesn't need any more toys." She sighed.

Christy laughed. "He can hardly fit on his cushion, Ellie, there's so many toys on there with him!"

Pet Life was a really big pet shop, with all sorts of animals. They even had a section for lizards and snakes and spiders, which was the only bit Ellie didn't like exploring.

The gerbils were in one corner, and Lucy led the way to them, half-running she

was so excited. She'd been looking forward to this for ages.

"Oh look!" she said, smiling. "See the golden ones! Aren't they beautiful?"

Ellie peered up at the cage, where two golden gerbils were nibbling peanuts, and staring back at the girls with sparkling black eyes. They were very sweet. She preferred dogs, but for a gentle person like Lucy, she could see that the gerbils were perfect.

One of the shop assistants helped Lucy choose her gerbils, and put them in a little travelling box. Lucy cradled it carefully, and they went to choose the cage – a huge one with lots of tubes and different rooms for the gerbils to explore. They'd almost filled the trolley with all the different stuff, when Lucy said, "There's just one more thing."

Her mum looked horrified. "More?"

"Not for us, Mum," Lucy explained. "In the dog section." She hurried off, and the others followed her as she searched carefully along the aisle.

"This!" she said at last, turning and holding out a knotted rope toy to Ellie. "Rascal hasn't got one of these, has he?" She beamed. "It's a thank-you present. If it wasn't for Rascal, that dog-food man would have given up and sent me home."

Ellie hugged her, very carefully so as not to squash the gerbils. "He'll love it."

"Do you like it, Rascal? Mmmm?"

Ellie was sitting on the sofa, playing tug of war with Rascal and his new rope toy. Mum had rolled her eyes when she'd seen it, but she hadn't really minded.

Lila suddenly yelped, and grabbed Ellie's hand. "Ellie, look! It's Lucy! And Rascal too, it's their ad. Mum! Dad! Max!" she called.

Ellie watched, giggling as Rascal rolled over, remembering how hard it had been to get him to do that. All that filming, squashed into one short ad now... "Watch, this is the pond bit!" she told Lila.

"Oh wow, poor Lucy!" Lila put her hand over her mouth, and then laughed. "Look at Rascal standing on the edge watching her!"

Rascal stopped chewing his toy and stared at the screen too. There was another dog in his living room, and it looked just like him. Only *he* was bigger! He eyed it suspiciously, then went back to his rope toy.

"You're a real TV star now, Rascal," Ellie told him proudly.

"Can I have his *pawtograph*?" Max asked, snorting with laughter, and Ellie groaned.

Rascal gave a huge yawn and climbed on to her lap, dragging the rope toy after him. Ellie gave him a hug. "I don't think you're even bothered about being famous, are you?" she asked him lovingly.

Rascal laid a protective paw over his new toy, in case that other dog came back and tried to snatch it, buried his nose in Ellie's elbow, and went to sleep.

Famous Ad Dogs
If you want to sell shoes, paint or loo paper, don't get a person to do it, get a pup!
Andrex Puppy
The adorable Andrex puppy is a Labrador retriever who runs away with the end of the company's brand of loo paper to demonstrate how long and strong it is.
The Dulux dog
Dulux has been using gorgeous Old English Sheepdogs to advertise its range of paint colours for the past 50 years. The current Dulux dog is called Spud. These dogs have a lot of hair: it takes four hours to groom Spud, and a further four to dry him after his bath!
Hush Puppies
This shoe brand is represented by a basset hound. Once, a salesman was having dinner in a southern U.S. state and learned that the fried cornballs he was eating were known as "hushpuppies", because farmers would toss the snacks to barking dogs to "hush" them. At the time, people called sore feet "barking dogs", and the salesman thought he could sell his comfortable shoes as something that would "hush" the pain away.
Coming soon:
My Naughty Little Puppy
Rascal and the Wedding
From best-selling author
HOLLY WEBB